The Three Wishes

A SPANISH FOLKTALE

Retold by Celenia Chévere

Illustrated by David Melendez

To my daughters Celene and Serena,
*who have been an inspiration to me—*C.C.

To my family
*Laura, Elijah, and Wes Ray. Mi Vida!—*D.M.

For information contact:
MONDO Publishing
One Plaza Road
Greenvale, New York 11548

Designed by Christy Hale
Production by Our House

Printed in Hong Kong by South China Printing Co. (1988) Ltd.
96 97 98 99 00 01   9 8 7 6 5 4 3 2 1

ISBN 1-57255-227-1

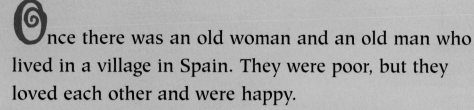

Once there was an old woman and an old man who lived in a village in Spain. They were poor, but they loved each other and were happy.

One evening the old woman was alone in their cottage, busy mending the old man's socks. While she was working, a fine grand lady came in.

"I would be so grateful if you would lend me your frying pan," said the fine grand lady. "My daughter will be married soon, and I am expecting guests from all over the country."

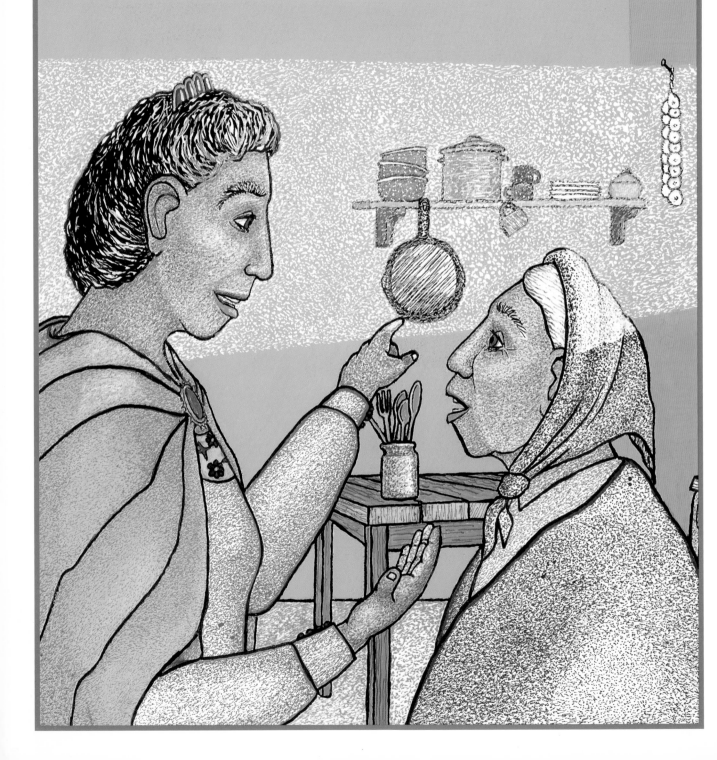

"Oh dear, yes! Of course you may borrow it," replied the old woman.

So the fine grand lady took the frying pan and thanked the old woman, promising to pay her well for the use of the pan.

A few days later the fine grand lady returned with the pan. Again she found the old woman alone.

"My deepest thanks for letting me use your frying pan," said the fine grand lady. "In return for your kindness you shall have three wishes."

With this the fine grand lady left. She disappeared so quickly that the old woman did not have time to ask her name or where she lived.

But now the old woman
had three wishes! She began to
think about what she would wish for.
    The old woman expected the old man
home soon. She decided to wait until he
arrived so he could help with the wishes.

In the meantime, the old woman wanted to cook a nice meal. Earlier she had been to her neighbor's cottage, and there she had seen a big juicy sausage, a chorizo.

"That was a beautiful chorizo," said the old
woman. "I wish I had one just like it for our meal."
And the next moment, a big fat chorizo appeared
on the table right before her.

The old woman was delighted. She was about to put the chorizo into the pan when the old man came in.

"Old man, old man," cried the old woman.
"Our troubles and hard work are over. I lent my
frying pan to a fine grand lady, and when she

returned it, she promised us three wishes.
And it's true. Just look at the chorizo I got
the moment I wished for it."

"You silly old woman," scolded the old man. "Why did you wish for a chorizo when you could have

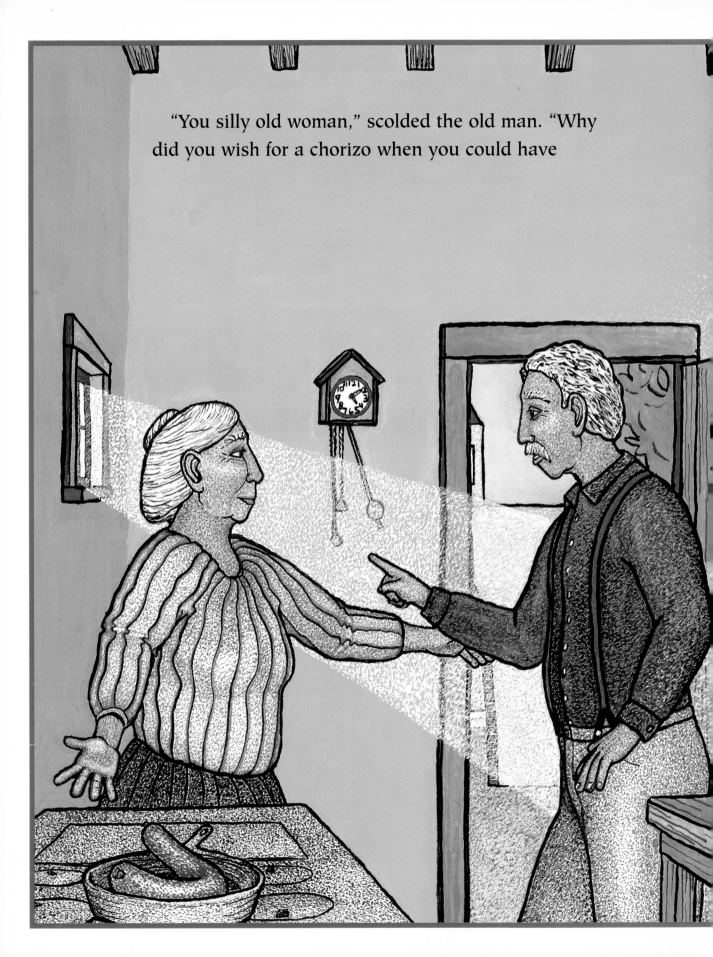

anything in the world? I wish that big fat chorizo
would stick to your nose."

At that the old woman began to cry, for sure enough, there was the chorizo hanging from her nose. She began pulling and tugging at it, but

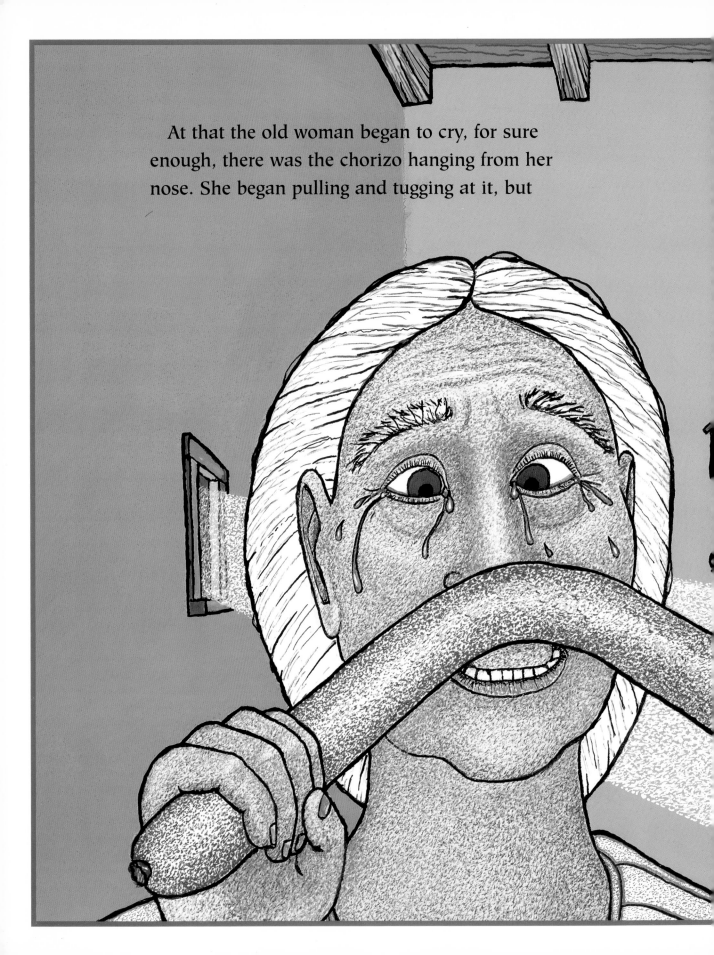

the more she pulled and tugged, the more it seemed to stick.

Oh what a sight it was—an old woman with a chorizo stuck to her nose!

"Ah dios mio, oh my goodness," cried the old woman. "How could you wish for such a terrible thing? All I wanted was something nice for us, and then . . . Ah dios mio, ah dios mio." The old woman continued to cry.

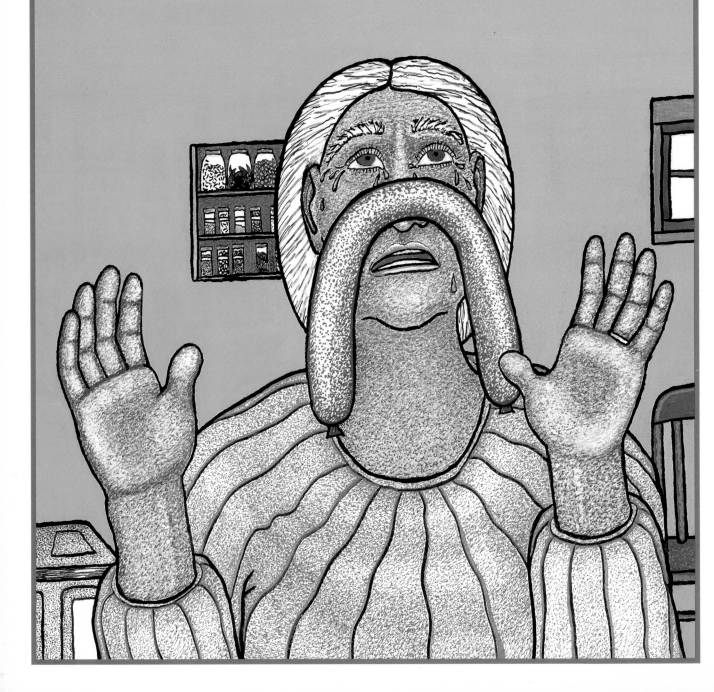

"We both made very foolish wishes," the old man said sadly. He put his arm around the old woman to comfort her, but she continued to cry and cry.

After a few moments, the old man decided to try pulling the chorizo from the old woman's nose. But the more he tugged, the harder the chorizo stuck. He pulled so hard the old woman's head seemed to be coming off her body.

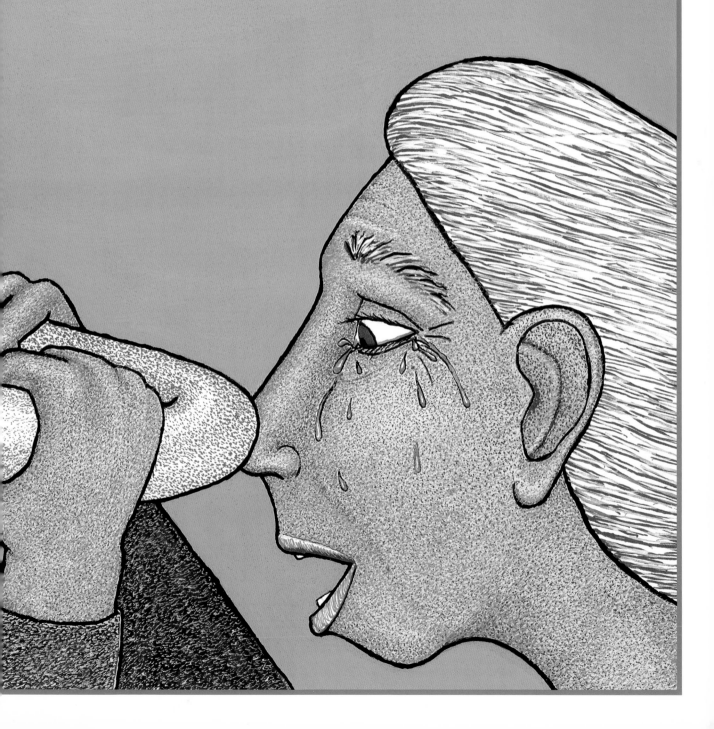

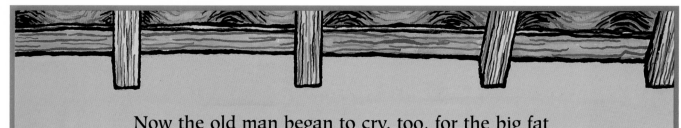

Now the old man began to cry, too, for the big fat chorizo was still hanging from the old woman's nose. Then he remembered the last wish.

"We have one wish left," the old man said to the old woman. "You wish for something."

"No, you wish for something," said the old woman, still crying.

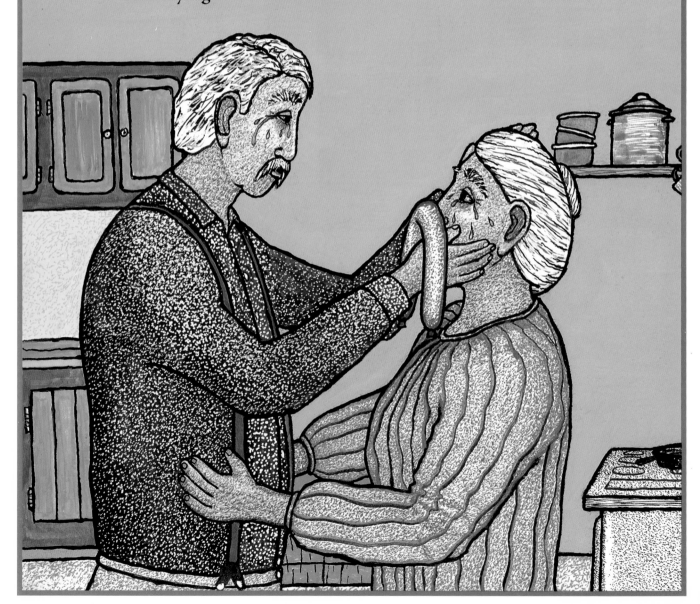

So the old man made the last wish. "I wish my wife was rid of that terrible chorizo," he said.

And in the next moment, the chorizo was gone.

The old man and the old woman were so happy they danced and danced around the room in great glee. And they agreed, a chorizo may be ever so nice when you have it in your mouth, but it would be quite a different thing to have one sticking to your nose all your life!